Lincolnshire

discover libraries

This book should be returned on or before the due date.

To renew or order library books please telephone 01522 782010
or visit https://lincolnshire.spydus.co.uk

You will require a Personal Identification Number.
Ask any member of staff for this.

The above does not apply to Reader's Group Collection Stock.

GRANDPA BERT

BERT

AND THE
Ghost Snatchers

MALORIE BLACKMAN

With illustrations by
Melanie Demmer

Barrington Stoke

Published in 2018 in Great Britain by
Barrington Stoke Ltd
18 Walker Street, Edinburgh, EH3 7LP

www.barringtonstoke.co.uk

This story was first published in a different form
as *Grandma Gertie's Haunted Handbag*
(Heinemann Young Books, 1996)

Text © 1996 Oneta Malorie Blackman
Illustrations © 2018 Melanie Demmer

A CIP catalogue record for this book is available
from the British Library upon request

ISBN: 978-1-78112-830-5

Printed in China by Leo

This book is in a super readable format for young readers
beginning their independent reading journey.

For Neil and Elizabeth

With much love

Contents

Chapter 1

Grandma Gertie Comes to Stay

Grandma Gertie was the oddest person Anna and her brother Kasper had ever seen.

It wasn't just her huge square glasses, or her hat with a real live parrot on it. (The parrot was winking at them as Grandma sat next to them on the back seat of the car.)

No, it was the odd way that Grandma Gertie's eyes gleamed. It was as if she had a secret that no one in the whole world knew except her. And the oddest thing of all was the way she kept patting her handbag. Pat! Pat! Pat! As if her handbag were a pet poodle.

"So how was your flight, Mum?" Dad asked Grandma from the front of the car.

"Fine as ripe peaches!" Grandma Gertie grinned. "I had four cups of tea and six buns!"

Kasper nudged Anna in the ribs. Anna nudged him back. She shifted along on the back seat of the car to put a bit more space between her and her strange grandma.

Then, without warning – PLOEUFF! BLOOP! BLOOOP! BLOOOOP!

"What on earth was that?" Dad said.
He pulled over to the side of the road
and stopped the car. They all got out.

"Rats! A flat tyre!" Dad groaned.
"And we're only ten minutes from
home!"

Dad inspected the tyre
as Grandma Gertie peered
over to look too.

"Don't worry, son," Grandma Gertie said to Dad. "It's only flat at the bottom." Dad gave Grandma Gertie a look, but she didn't seem to notice.

"Dad, can I help you fix the tyre?" Kasper asked.

Anna wanted to help too, but Grandma Gertie grabbed her arm and started to pull her along the High Street.

Anna grabbed Kasper's hand – no way did Anna want to be alone with her very odd grandma. And off they all went together.

"Don't mind me!" Dad called after them. "I'll manage!"

Grandma Gertie looked up and down the street as she raced along.

"We'll have to be quick," Grandma said. "I think someone's after me."

"After you?" Kasper asked. "Who's after you?"

"Never mind that now," Grandma Gertie hissed. Then she yanked Anna and Kasper into an alley. "How are the two of you with duppies?" she asked.

"Duppies?" Anna was puzzled. "What's a duppy?"

"A ghost, dear," Grandma Gertie said. "That's what we call them in Barbados. How would you like to meet a duppy?"

"Er ... I don't think so ..." Kasper said, and took a hasty step away.

'She's bonkers! I knew it!' Anna thought.

Grandma Gertie took another quick look around. Then she clicked the clasp on her handbag.

Anna's mouth fell wide open and stayed wide open! Kasper moved in for a closer look, then gasped. His eyes were as big as the head lights on their car.

There was a face staring up out of
the handbag. And attached to that face
was the folded-up body of a ghost!

Chapter 2
Hello, Bert!

"Say hello to your Grandpa Bert then!"
Grandma Gertie said with a grin.

Anna stared. Up until that moment,
she'd thought that her Grandma was
joking with them – or that she was as
nutty as a lorry full of peanut butter!

But the ghost just smiled at Anna, then turned to Grandma Gertie.

"Are we in England then?" the ghost asked.

"Yes, Bert – we are!" Grandma Gertie replied.

Grandpa Bert jumped out of the bag and dusted himself off. "That's better," he said. "I hate travelling by handbag!"

"You ... you're a ghost!" Anna
squeaked.

"A real live ghost!" Kasper squealed.

"A real ghost in the flesh!" Grandpa Bert said as he winked at them both.

"I wanted to meet you before you got much older," he went on. "These days, most grown-ups and even some children can't see us ghosts, because they don't believe in us. I wanted to meet you before you stopped believing in me!"

"I tried to buy Bert a plane ticket, but they wouldn't let me," Grandma Gertie told Anna and Kasper. "I even showed them Bert's passport, but the staff at the airport couldn't see him and so they thought I was a proper odd-bod!"

Grandma Gertie leaned close to Anna and Kasper, and peered over the top of her huge square glasses. "I mean, do I look like an odd-bod to you?"

"No, Grandma." Anna and Kasper shook their heads, but they crossed their fingers firmly behind their backs.

"Exactly!" Grandma Gertie said with a shrug. "So the only way was to bring Bert in my handbag."

"Grandpa Bert! Grandpa Bert!" Grandma Gertie's parrot shouted over and over. "Grandpa Bert! Grandpa Bert!"

"Mix-A-Lot, hush up!" Grandma Gertie said as she held her parrot's beak shut.

A parrot called Mix-A-Lot and the ghost of Grandpa Bert!

Anna pinched herself, just in case she was dreaming. She wasn't!

"Now, Kasper and Anna," Grandma Gertie said, "I want you two to take good care of Grandpa Bert. He's not safe in my handbag any more. I'm sure I'm being followed."

"You are?" Anna said. "Why? Who's following you?" She looked around.

"I don't know. I didn't think the machines at the airport could detect ghosts, but maybe they can." Grandma Gertie frowned. "From the time we left the airport, I've had the strangest feeling ..."

"We'd better get out of this alley for a start," Grandpa Bert said. "So, where do you want me, Anna?"

"Huh?" Anna was puzzled.

"Well, I can't travel with Gertie," Grandpa Bert explained. "If someone is following her, then it isn't safe." Bert shook his head. "So where do you want me? And don't say in your pocket!"

Before Anna could think of an answer, she heard the sound of footsteps coming along the pavement towards them.

"Quick! Quick!" Grandma Gertie said, and she hopped from foot to foot.

Anna took off her hat. "Grandpa Bert, in here – hurry!"

Bert vanished into Anna's hat like he was a genie getting back into its bottle. Anna pulled her hat back on.

"Ow!" Bert protested. "OW!"

"Shush!" Anna and Kasper said.

The footsteps grew louder as they got closer and closer ...

Anna looked around. There was nothing behind them but a brick wall. There was nothing in front of them. In fact, there was no way out apart from towards the street, towards the footsteps ...

Chapter 3

A Pencil and Two Wild Eyebrows

Anna held her breath.

"Oh, there you are! I wondered where you'd all got to."

Anna let out a huge sigh of relief. It was only Dad.

They all walked back to the car.
Dad and Grandma Gertie led the way,
followed by Anna and Kasper.

"Let's see Grandpa Bert again,"
Kasper whispered.

Anna tipped up her hat a bit.

"There's a cold breeze!" Grandpa Bert
moaned.

Anna pulled her hat down tight onto her head. She had the jitters still. Was Grandma Gertie really being followed?

"A real live ghost!" Kasper said. He still couldn't get over it.

Anna was about to tell her brother to shush when she saw something odd on the other side of the street.

A man and woman were walking at the exact same speed as Anna and Kasper.

The woman was as tall and thin as a pencil and the man had very wild bushy eyebrows. They looked like a big bush growing on his face.

But the real reason Anna spotted them was because the man and woman were staring at Anna and her family and not looking where they were going.

Anna nudged Kasper and pointed to the strange man and woman. Then she ran up to Grandma.

"Grandma, look!" Anna whispered. "There! Across the street!"

"Hush, child. I can see them," Grandma Gertie said. "Let's get in the car!"

At that moment, Anna knew they were all in BIG trouble.

Chapter 4
The Stolen Handbag

They were soon in the car and on their way home again, but Anna didn't feel at all safe. From the look on Kasper's face, he felt the same.

But Dad was busy chatting away to Grandma Gertie, and she was chatting back as if nothing was wrong.

"All I've seen of England so far is the inside of Gertie's handbag and the top of your head," Grandpa Bert grumbled from under Anna's hat.

"Shush!" Anna told him.

"Anna, why are you telling everyone to shush?" Dad said with a frown.

"Er ... I wasn't," Anna said. "I was talking to myself."

"I love talking to myself!" Grandma Gertie smiled. "It's such a great way to have an interesting chat."

Dad just shook his head and kept on driving.

At last they were home.

But just as Grandma Gertie set foot on the pavement, the Pencil Woman sprinted up and grabbed her handbag. Then the woman sprinted around the corner.

Seconds later, Anna heard the screech of tyres as a car sped away.

It all happened so fast that there was no time to do anything. Everyone just stood there feeling shocked for a moment. Then Dad dashed around the corner. Soon he ran back, his face hot with anger.

"The car was going too fast for me to read the number plate," he yelled.

"Don't worry about it, son," Grandma Gertie said with a shrug. "My handbag was empty anyway."

"Empty?" Dad asked.

"Yep! My passport and my purse are safe. See!" And Grandma Gertie lifted up her hat. There on her head were her purse, passport and a packet of chocolate raisins.

"Mum, why have you got all that stuff under your hat?" Dad asked.

"There was no room in my handbag," Grandma Gertie said.

Dad frowned. "But you just said your handbag was empty," he said.

"So I did, dear. So I did." And Grandma Gertie walked up the garden path to the house.

Now Dad looked totally puzzled.

Kasper stood on tiptoes to talk to Anna's hat. "Are you all right up there, Grandpa Bert?" he whispered.

"Anna's hair is tickling my nose and I've got a crick in my neck," Grandpa Bert said. "But apart from that I'm fine!"

"How can a ghost get a crick in his neck?" Kasper asked. "You don't have bones or muscles to get sore."

"Kasper, who on earth are you talking to?" Dad asked.

"No one," Kasper said. "No one at all!"

Dad shook his head. "You're talking to yourself as well? It must be catching!"

Chapter 5
Under Anna's Hat

As Dad followed Grandma up to the house, Anna took off her hat.

Grandpa Bert popped his head up and stretched his neck. "Ah, that's better," he said.

"It's lucky you weren't in Grandma's handbag," Anna murmured.

"I know," Grandpa Bert said. "I heard what happened."

"Maybe Pencil Woman was after Grandma Gertie's money?" Kasper said.

"I don't think so," Grandpa Bert said, and he shook his head. "She was after me, I'm sure of it."

Grandpa Bert popped back under Anna's hat as Mum opened the front door. Grandma Gertie and Mum gave each other a BIG hug. Then they all went inside and into the kitchen. Mum put the kettle on and Anna put her hat down on the table so that Grandpa Bert could have a rest.

"Guess what happened?" Dad said to Mum. He was still very angry. "Some woman ran past Grandma Gertie and stole her handbag."

"You're joking!" Mum said. She couldn't believe it.

"I'm going to phone the police right now," Dad said.

"There's no need to do that," Grandma Gertie told him, as calm as anything. "Like I said, my handbag was empty."

"I'm still going to call the police," Dad said.

"Too right!" Mum was shocked. "What's the world coming to?"

The doorbell rang and they all jumped in surprise.

"I'll get it," Anna said as she went to open the front door.

"Mum! Dad! Look!" Anna called out.

Everyone ran to the door. Grandma Gertie's handbag was there on the step. Anna picked it up and handed it to Grandma.

"Why on earth did the thief bring it back?" Mum said.

They all stood and looked at the bag when ...

SLAM! went the kitchen door as someone banged it shut.

Anna and Kasper looked at each other.

"Grandpa Bert!" they shouted.

Everyone ran back to the kitchen – but they were too late.

Anna's hat and Grandpa Bert had gone.

Chapter 6
A Bike for Everyone

"Quick!" shouted Anna. She and Kasper ran out of the side gate and onto the street. "There's Wild Eyebrows running towards a car!"

And on Wild Eyebrows' head was Anna's hat! His head was so big and Anna's hat was so small that it looked like a pea sitting on top of a mountain!

Pencil Woman stood next to the car, beckoning at Wild Eyebrows to run faster.

"They've got Grandpa Bert!" Kasper yelled. "What can we do?"

"Bert!" Grandma Gertie wailed. "They've got my Bert!"

"The bikes! Get the bikes!" Anna called out. "We've got to stop them."

Kasper and Anna ran round to the shed for their bikes.

Grandma Gertie was just behind them. "Whose bike is this?" she asked.

"That's Dad's bike," Kasper said.

"It'll do!" Grandma Gertie cried. She hopped onto Dad's bike.

"But, Grandma, you can't ..." Anna began.

"There's no time to argue," Grandma Gertie interrupted. "If we don't hurry, we'll lose them."

"Mum, what are you doing on my bike?" Dad asked. "Will someone please tell me what's going on?"

"We're just going for a nice bike ride before dinner, son," Grandma Gertie said.

And then she was off!

Chapter 7
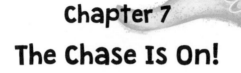
The Chase Is On!

Grandma Gertie pedalled down the path so fast that Mum and Dad had to jump out of her way.

Kasper and Anna were close behind. They all rode out of the front gate and down the road after the car.

As they turned the corner, the traffic lights at the end of the road turned to green. The car pulled away from the lights and turned left.

"They're getting away," Grandma Gertie called out.

"Oh no they're not!" Anna said.

Anna and Kasper pedalled even harder. Grandma Gertie found it hard to keep up with them.

It was lucky that the traffic was so bad that the getaway car couldn't go very fast. Soon, Anna and Kasper were catching it up.

"Hold on, Grandpa Bert," Anna yelled. "We're coming!"

"If they get out of town and away from the traffic, we'll never keep up with them," Kasper shouted to Anna.

And so, Anna and Kasper pedalled faster than they'd ever pedalled before.

But Grandma Gertie had to stop for a rest.

"Never mind me," she called out. "I'll catch up."

Up ahead, the car turned left again and Anna and Kasper raced after it. They were just in time to see the car vanish down a drive lined with trees.

The two children pedalled down the drive and there, at the end of it, stood the getaway car. It was empty.

Chapter 8
Ghost Works

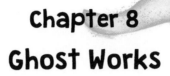

"Look where we are!" said Anna as she jumped off her bike.

They were outside a huge house. And above the front door were the words – GHOST WORKS.

"Come on, Kasper!" Anna said. "Let's rescue Grandpa Bert."

Anna bent low and then she dashed across to the corner of the house. Kasper did the same. Anna kept flat to the wall and moved down the side of the house. She peeped into every window. At the second window at the back of the house, she stopped and beckoned to Kasper.

"Shush!" Anna whispered, and they both peered in the window.

The room was filled with strange glass tubes. Each tube was as high as the ceiling and had a big pipe coming out of it. And in each tube there was a ghost!

In the glass tube near to the door was ... Grandpa Bert.

And there was Wild Eyebrows looking in the tube at him.

"LET ME OUT!" Grandpa Bert yelled as he banged on the glass. But it was no good.

"You're wasting your time!" Wild Eyebrows laughed.

"Who are you?" Grandpa Bert asked. "Why did you bring me here?"

"We're the Ghost Works Spectral Agency," said Wild Eyebrows. "At your service! Our secret monitors at the airport showed us that Gertie had a ghost in her handbag."

"But what are you going to do with me?" Grandpa Bert asked.

Wild Eyebrows smiled – an evil, oily smile. "You're going to work for us like all the other ghosts in here," he said. "You can work as a spy, or scare our enemies, or go on missions that are too dangerous for living people. The ghosts who work for us are always busy."

"I'll never work for you," Grandpa Bert yelled. "Never!"

"That's what all our ghosts say at first, but you'll soon change your mind," Wild Eyebrows said in a soft, creepy voice. "Not that you have any choice. We've got you now and we're never going to let you go. Ever!"

And, with a horrid cackle, Wild Eyebrows left the room.

Chapter 9
In a Glass Prison

The moment Wild Eyebrows left, Anna pushed up the window. She and Kasper scrambled over the window sill and ran up to Grandpa Bert in his tall glass tube.

"Hold on, Grandpa Bert," Anna whispered. "We'll soon have you out of that horrid glass prison."

"No! You need to leave," Grandpa Bert told them. "Those Ghost Works crooks will be back soon."

"No way!" Kasper said. "We're not leaving you here."

"Too right!" Anna agreed.

"Let me out too ..." another ghost wailed in a spooky voice.

"Oh, please save me ..." wailed another one.

"Help! Please help!" a third ghost wailed.

"How?" Kasper asked. "Just tell us what to do ..."

"Press the button on that control panel over there," said a sharp voice. It belonged to a ghost who looked like Queen Elizabeth I.

"Careful!" said a ghost dressed like a ragged chimney sweep. "If you press the wrong button, the alarm will go off."

Kasper looked around. All the pipes from the glass tubes led to a control panel on the other side of the room. He raced over. The control panel had lots of dials and levers and buttons – but none of them had labels.

'Oh no!' Kasper thought. 'What shall I do?'

Then he saw it! A single cable behind the control panel led to a plug.

Kasper bent down, took a deep breath and pulled the plug out of the wall.

BOOM!

All the lights on the control panel went out and all the doors to the glass tubes sprang open.

"Let's go!" Anna said.

"But what about Wild Eyebrows and Pencil Woman?" Kasper asked.

"Don't worry!" a pirate ghost said. "My cutlass will soon sort them out ..."

Chapter 10
Home Time

It was time to escape!

Grandpa Bert wrapped himself around Kasper's neck like a spooky scarf. Then Kasper dived out of the window, followed by Anna.

"All this fun – and I've only been in the country a few hours!" Grandpa Bert

said. "I think I'll stay for a bit longer!
This is great!"

Anna and Kasper raced over to the bikes. And who was there but Grandma Gertie!

"We need to get out of here before Wild Eyebrows and Pencil Woman see that Grandpa Bert and all the other ghosts are missing," Anna said.

But it was too late!

The Ghost Works front door burst open and out ran Wild Eyebrows and Pencil Woman.

Anna's heart sank. They'd never get away now – not if these two crooks chased them in their car. But Wild Eyebrows and Pencil Woman didn't head for their car – they rushed the other way down the drive.

A cloud of VERY angry ghosts was hot on their heels!

"I think that's the last we'll see of those two crooks for a long, long time," Grandma Gertie said with a laugh.

"Long, long time!" Mix-A-Lot squawked, from Grandma Gertie's hat.

Anna and Kasper grinned and gave each other a high five.

"Home time," Anna said as she got on her bike.

"Home in time for dinner," Kasper said.

"Oh, don't talk about dinner!" Grandpa Bert said with a sigh. "I'm so hungry after all this excitement, but ghosts can't eat a thing! I'd give anything for the taste of a sweet mango or some juicy grapes or a slice of pineapple or ..."

Anna, Kasper, Grandma Gertie and Mix-A-Lot looked at each other. They turned to Bert and all said together, "Shush!"

But they might as well have been talking to themselves.

Because all the way home Grandpa
Bert did nothing but talk about what
he'd like to eat for dinner – if only he
wasn't a ghost!

Our books are tested
for children and young people by
children and young people.

Thanks to everyone who consulted on
a manuscript for their time and effort in
helping us to make our books better
for our readers.